39 Hours

A Short Dark Thriller

By
Robert Schobernd

Novels by the Author

In The Irrevocable Change trilogy
Book One – **The Assassin is Created**
Book Two - **The Assassin Evolves**
Book Three - **The Assassin's Revenge**

*****

Also by this author,
The Blonde Heiress
A Novella Introducing Carter A.
Johnson

Five Carter A. Johnson and Kate Menke
Thrillers
The Dogtrot Murder
Cape Abigail
The Three Monkeys
Acceptance First: Revenge Second
Predictable Consequences

*****

Two Zombie Apocalypse Thrillers
Outnumbered
Running to Escape

*****

A Second Chance Love Story
Choices: Karolyn's Story

And now settle back with a drink and a snack and enjoy,

59 Hours

Damn it's hot. I'm sweaty, dusty, and probably stink, but I should be almost there. That's got to be Cousin Mikey's farm at the top of the next rise. Just one more damn hill to climb in this damn heat. This suitcase I'm lugging is too heavy. I shouldn't have packed so much, but I didn't want to leave anything behind. I can't go back, that's for damn sure.

The bottom of my foot will be black from the scraps of newspaper I put over the hole in the thin leather sole. Damned rocks have probably bruised my foot; it sure hurts like it's bruised. Should've stopped a mile back and put my work boots on.

Sure as hell hope he's home. Huh! Of course, he's home. Dirt farmers can't afford to leave even for a night. His run-down old farm buildings look worse than the ones I left except his barn is still standing and that's the biggest thing I see different. Ain't much to look at. Just another rundown ole farm with the dirt turning to dust.

If that damn old Chevrolet pickup hadn't quit, I'd have been here at sunup this morning. And I wouldn't be walking. Dammed old truck.

That kid on the bus needed his butt tanned. Yelled, ran up and down the aisle, and constantly whined. Mother's leather strap would have got his attention. It got mine often enough. I'm tired, didn't get any sleep on the whole four-hour bus ride.

Damn that old Chevrolet truck.

What an experience this has been. First the truck's engine locked up. The guy who gave me a lift to town looked under the hood and said it was out of oil. Then after I bought a ticket at the bus station, the driver put me off in the middle of nowhere. Nary a shade tree close by to cool off under.

Finally, that baldheaded old fool stopped to give me a lift. What a windbag, blowhard he was. Bet his wife would have raised nine kinds of hell if she'd seen him staring at my tits and legs. He shouldn't have stared like that. I only pulled my dress up near my belly and unbuttoned the bodice because it's so hot. He knew that. The old fool even slobbered tobacco juice down his chin until it dripped on his ratty white shirt. It's a wonder he didn't come right out and proposition me. He surely dropped enough dirty hints.

I wonder what it would be like to have sex for money. It shouldn't be much different than for free with boys at school.

Frances reached the dirt and gravel lane and trudged toward the ramshackle two-story farmhouse. When she got to the shade cast by twin ancient soft maples, she set the thin, tan paperboard suitcase on edge in the dry grass and sat on it. The temperature under the tree had to be ten or more degrees cooler, and she lingered enjoying the occasional slight breeze that dried the moisture from her skin and cooled her dress. She thought of second Cousin Mikey. She hadn't seen him in over ten years. She'd have been nine then and he would have been sixteen.

She knew it was Wednesday and looking at where the sun was in the cloudless blue sky guessed it must be about two in the afternoon. Her stomach rumbled as if to notify her it was well past lunchtime.

The house looked even worse up close than it had from the far ridge.

White paint had chipped away leaving most boards bare and gray and several siding boards were gone. She stood, walked to the porch, climbed the steps, placed the battered suitcase on the bare, weathered porch deck and knocked on the screen door. She knocked louder and longer. Still no answer. The inside door stood open so either someone was home or would return shortly. She yelled, "Ha, anybody home?" Maybe Cousin Mikey was in the barn or out in a field.

Two weathered straight-backed chairs on the porch faced the road. Frances sat on the nearest one and fidgeted to kill time, unsure of what to do next. Her fingers nervously drummed against her legs as she listened for any sound of life. *Mother would know what to do. She'd decide instantly and do something. She always knew what was proper to do and I was always told what I'd done was wrong. Always.* The thought caused her to think of Daddy. She thought of him often, but it had gotten harder to remember what he'd looked like. He'd called her his sweet little angel.

The buildings on this farm were in worse shape than Mother's. These were bare of paint and the roofs on most sagged like swaybacked old horses ready for the glue factory. The livestock barn looked small, much smaller than the one at home had been. But then the house was smaller than Mother's too.

"Who are you? What do you want?"

Frances jumped at the sound of the loud, deep, gruff male voice. She bolted off the chair and turned toward the door. A figure stood in the dim parlor away from the door. A man, maybe taller and slimmer than she remembered Mikey, looked at her. She couldn't see his features clearly through the dusty screen.

"I'm Cousin Frances, your mother's first cousin."

He didn't reply.

As her eyes adjusted to the gloom, she vaguely saw him in the dim interior room. He appeared bigger than she'd imagined and that surprised her. His features were different, not handsome by any means, but not as plain and stupid looking as she remembered. Her cousins used to call him little pig eyes. Of course, she was just a kid the last time she saw him. But she thought he looked a lot different.

"You are Cousin Mikey, aren't you?"

"I prefer to be called Michael. Why are you here?"

"I left home to live on my own. I'm going to get a job and support myself."

"Go away." After uttering the single terse comment, the man turned and walked off.

Frances advanced, put her face nearly to the screen and yelled after him, "You're rude and ill-mannered. You could at least put me up for the night before I leave. We are family after all. You could maybe even give me a ride to town in the morning. You could do that, you know!"

A minute passed before Michael returned with long purposeful strides and stood silent as he stared at her for several seconds. "You can stay the night. I'll feed you then haul you to town in the truck in the morning. You'll sleep in the room at the top of the stairs on the left."

She grabbed the suitcase and stepped through the doorway as he walked into the kitchen at the back of the house. A swarm of flies entered with her before the wood screen door slammed loudly behind them. The stairway was steep, narrow, dark, and hot. She set the suitcase on a chair, opened it, set her boots beside the bed then went back downstairs. The second-floor bedrooms were even hotter than the first-floor parlor.

In the kitchen, she tried to make small talk, but Michael ignored her. He sat at the table and drank from a brown beer bottle while he glared at her through squinted eyes. He was sullen and immersed in private thought. A slight grin appeared and then in an instant was gone. It came and went so quickly Frances wondered if she had imagined it.

"I'm hungry. I haven't eaten since early this morning."

He pointed. "There's a stick of small bologna in the fridge, store-bought bread in the breadbox. Cold water is in the green refrigerator jar, glasses are behind that door. Refill the jar from the bucket if you use from it."

Before she turned to the refrigerator, she had noted Michael was tall, lean, muscular, and remembered his fleeting grin had a nasty almost mean quality. He needed a shave, and definitely was not handsome. His blue work pants looked clean, but the once white undershirt was worn and dingy. The twin shoulder straps were frayed at the edges of the cotton material and were more stained than the rest of the shirt.

As Frances moved across the room, Michael saw she was overweight by twenty pounds, a lot for her medium height. She was plain and frowzy. He'd smelled her body odor as she walked by him. Her flowery printed cotton dress was rumpled, thin and faded from many harsh washings. Her brown hair was unkempt and tangled and she wore no makeup. He bet she was never pretty or popular in school. *Definitely not my type. But, maybe? She just might do it with the right coaching.* He stood and without explanation left the house through the kitchen door.

Through the window Frances saw Michael walk two hundred feet to the dilapidated old barn that retained just a reddish hint of the paint that had covered it years ago when it was a new addition to the farm.

She couldn't understand why Michael was so guarded; after all, they were kin. While she ate a sandwich, she thought of the last time she'd seen Mikey. It had to be a family reunion when her Daddy was still alive. Mikey had changed a lot, plus he used to be friendly. Back then he was the only cousin she could talk with. The others always made fun of her for being overweight and clumsy and called her names, mean hurtful names. She hadn't liked them and wanted to hit them, but they were bigger, tougher, and meaner than her. A smile formed as she realized she'd gotten bigger, tougher and meaner too. A lot tougher and meaner.

She wiped crumbs off the table, put the food away, and then roamed the house. Upstairs were four bedrooms off a central hallway, two to a side. On a chest of drawers in his bedroom she saw a picture of her first cousin, Emma, Mikey's mother. His bed was rumpled just as he'd left it when he'd gotten up that morning. Sweat dampened her again as she made Michael's bed just like Mother had always demanded she make her own. The spread had to be pulled tight as a drum skin and the corners tucked neatly.

On the first floor, Frances walked through an empty, unused room in the back, a dining room, the parlor, and the kitchen. The walls and ceilings of the whole house were covered with cheap wallpaper. Some of it was worn bare by hands and scrapes, and some hung loose at the seams. The paper at home was of better quality and Mother routinely reglued what loosened with a flour and water paste. Mother had been a stickler for everything being neat and clean.

Bored, she left the hot, dark, stuffy house. Behind the kitchen she looked at the vegetable garden. Most plants had either died from the drought or had wilted. She found a galvanized bucket, pumped water from the well, and watered the plants she thought could be saved. Behind the garden sat a chicken coop where seven hens and one scraggly rooster roamed outside it. They pecked at the dirt for bugs or bits of cracked corn when not chasing and pecking at each other. She was surprised not to see or hear any livestock. All the farms she knew of had cows and pigs, and most had a team of horses or mules. Some even had guinea hens flittering around the yard and roosting in the trees. *Mikey doesn't even have cats or dogs getting underfoot. That's strange, never heard of a farm without animals.* Before going back inside, she ignored the flies and mud daubers and used the two-hole outhouse. She looked at the women's clothing pages in the Montgomery Ward catalog with longing and then used the hardware pages to wipe. She stood and realized that was the same way she'd always done at home. But that was....

In the kitchen she found a washcloth, soap and a granite wash pan. With water from a bucket on the sink she moved to the pantry and gave herself a quick wash from head to foot. It felt good to feel clean, even if the clothes she put back on were stiff with dried sweat.

Soon afterward, Frances watched Michael return. He entered the house through the parlor and tossed a coiled length of rope in the corner by the stairs. Mother would never have allowed that.

In the kitchen, Michael opened a beer. "Frances, you want a beer?" His tone startled her; he sounded friendly. "I've got fried pork chops and some biscuits left from last night. Why don't you pick a mess of green beans from the garden, if there's any left on the plants? You can boil them with some new potatoes from the cellar and cut a few slices of bacon off that cured slab in the refrigerator to flavor them. I'll pick a couple tomatoes and we'll have the fixings for dinner."

Frances found enough beans for several meals and cooked them in a cast-iron pot. She used the old wood fired stove outside on the back open porch to keep the heat out of the kitchen.

During supper she asked about livestock.

Michael leaned back and slipped both thumbs through the undershirt shoulder straps. "They had to be sold because we couldn't afford to keep them. Didn't get hardly anything for them. Everybody else has the same problems. Pasture grass is dead and store-bought feed is expensive. The wheat harvest was terrible, so to conserve cash they had to go. You asked before if I was your Cousin Mikey. I'm not. My name is Michael Smith. I'm Mikey's partner. I bought a half share in the farm three years ago. Mikey went up North to look at a combine we need to buy. Our old one is worn out, and we've got to replace it. He'll be back in three or four days. I apologize for being in a bad temper when you arrived. I'm not usually that way, but this weather is wearing on me." He smiled and she believed him.

Michael helped with the dishes after supper. They joked and laughed, then each grabbed a beer and moved to the parlor. Frances had only tasted beer a few times before and didn't care for the bitterness, but she didn't want to sound like a child by refusing. They sat on opposite ends of the massive black leather couch.

She asked, "I guess you're from this area?"

"No, I'm from the Northern end of the state. After I got out of the Army, I drifted from town to town looking for work hoping to find a place to settle. Luckily, I met Mikey and used my mustering out pay to buy into the farm. We did good my first year here."

They continued to get to know each other while they drank more beer. After the second one Frances felt a bit lightheaded.

"Tell me about Mikey's cousin, who are you?" Michael asked.

"Me? I don't know. I'm nineteen. I dropped out of high school before my senior year started because Mother needed me to help work the farm. My daddy died of the TB when I was twelve. Mother is very independent and kept the farm going without a man. It was just her and me. She sold it last week and moved to town. I decided it was time to be on my own. I have a little money saved and hope I can find a job. Maybe as a store clerk or a waitress in a restaurant. What about you?"

"I'm thirty-four and don't care to live with my kin folk. Like I said, I had a little money when I got out of the Army and stopped here. I was married while I was in the Army, but my wife cheated on me while I was gone. Luckily there weren't any kids. We're divorced now, but I plan to find another woman. One I can trust and start over with. I was too young when I married and picked the wrong woman. Now I know better."

They talked late into the evening and Michael gradually moved closer each time he went for more beers.

The more they talked the more Frances decided she liked Michael, really liked him. He flirted and slid next to her on the sofa to touch and joke. She knew she was having trouble talking because her words sounded slurred even to her. Later they engaged in mild kissing and necking. It seemed like they laughed and talked for hours, and after another beer Frances was woozy. As the night air finally cooled, they were into heavy necking and groping. Well after dark they went upstairs and made love before she passed out and both went to sleep.

Michael nudged Frances awake. "Come on sleepyhead, we've got a full day's work ahead of us. She felt something poke at her belly and reached out for him. She raised her head, and it hurt. Michael was smiling so she didn't mention the headache she had from the previous night's beer drinking. They kissed and she pulled him close. He laughed and said, "Well, I guess we can take time-out for this."

After making love again, he told her. "You can stay, but only because I like you. Mikey will need to agree with me, but that shouldn't be a problem if you're my girlfriend." Frances saw a big grin on his face and knew he'd fallen for her. He wanted her to be his girlfriend. She was ecstatic. Her first real boyfriend.

Michael got out of bed, grabbed his clothes and left the room. Several minutes later he returned. "Put these clothes on and wear your boots. But bring your girl clothes and stuff along, too."

She was puzzled, "Why do you want me to dress like a man?"

"It's a surprise. Just go along with me on this." He pulled her close and kissed her, then grinned and turned to leave. "I'll be outside. Yell when breakfast is ready."

Frances dug through her suitcase and removed clean clothes. She couldn't believe her good fortune. She's been gone from home only two days and had a boyfriend. Mother wouldn't believe it. She'd said no decent man would ever want her silly, lazy daughter.

Michael crossed to the barn and smirked. *It's easier than I thought it would be. The poor girl is not only naive she's dumber than snake shit.*

They each smiled a lot during breakfast. Frances made a pot of strong coffee to wash down sausage links, fried eggs and potatoes, and fresh baked biscuits.

Between bites Michael complimented her. "Somebody sure taught you how to cook good food. There hasn't been cooking like this since I got here three years ago. Mikey's a terrible cook and I'm not much better."

"Mother taught me to cook. I made stuff so often I remember most of her recipes in my head."

Neither mentioned the previous night and confined their small talk to the weather and what needed to be done around the farm to make it profitable when the drought ended.

After they cleared the table Michael said, "Leave the dishes. I have a surprise for you, and we need to leave, or we'll be too late."

Frances slammed the door on the green truck and Michael backed the Studebaker pickup from the shed. When she again wanted to know where they were headed and what they were going to do he continued to joke about having a big surprise for her. During the two-hour drive she talked most of the time, but he managed to inject words she longed to hear.

"I'm a lucky guy," he said. "I have a good partner in a farm that we'll make a showplace when the weather gets better. And since you've showed up, I feel I may have the woman to stand with me while that happens. I like you. This might make you blush, but you were something in bed last night. I like having you around. How does that fit with your feelings?"

Frances's eyes lit with affection. "I'm so happy I decided to visit Mikey. If I'd gone anywhere else, I wouldn't have met you. Last night was wonderful, and I'm not embarrassed about making love to a wonderful man." *Mother would kill me if she knew what I did and that I'm not ashamed of it. Or rather she would have.*

They continued for a short time before Michael turned at a side road that intersected with the highway. Three cars were parked on the edge of the gravel road. He parked the truck behind the last car.

Michael turned to Frances. He was somber and his voice was low. "Look, times are hard on the farm. We're just barely hanging on, and we lose ground every day with this damned drought going on and on. I know it will end, but who knows how long that will be. Mikey and I had to do something to hang on or we'd both have lost everything we've worked hard for."

Frances listened intently and wondered where the conversation was going.

"I need your help until Mikey gets back. It started as Mikey's idea, and I rejected it at first. Finally, he convinced me, and I went along. I know it's wrong, but to supplement the money we lose on the farm we've turned to robbing banks."

Her jaw dropped and a shocked expression froze on her face. "You and Cousin Mikey rob banks? You can't do that! You'll get caught and go to jail, or you may both get shot."

"Frances, this year's wheat harvest was real poor, even worse than last year's harvest. We couldn't pay the note at the bank with the meager profit, so we used the money we stole.

Mikey took the rest of the money to buy a different combine. The old one is worn out and so is the tractor. We can't afford new machinery, so we're buying used ones in good condition. A farm up North was foreclosed by the bank. The equipment is only three years old. It's being auctioned tomorrow, and Mikey is hoping to buy it. We've got to have decent equipment, or we'll go belly up and lose everything. You understand that, don't you? That's where you come in. I need you to help me rob a bank this morning. I can't do it by myself, or I wouldn't ask."

"Oh my God! No. I can't do that. Mother would have a fit if I were caught."

"You've got to do this for us, you, me, and Mikey. We're all in this together. Do this for us or we don't have a future. You'll just have to get out of the truck and go away. Mikey and I are committed to saving our farm and our future and if you aren't willing to sacrifice too...."

Slowly and softly he said, "If you want to be my woman, you've got to help me. I like you and we'll be a great team. We need to plan for our long-term relationship. And that means we need to save the farm from the bank taking it over."

"But, I can't do this. I don't know how to rob a bank!"

"There's nothing to it. We'll have nylon stockings over our head so nobody can see our face to identify us. I'll do most of the work and all the talking. You'll stay in front of the teller's windows and watch customers, so they don't try to leave. All you'll need to do is yell at them to stay down, or you'll shoot them."

"Shoot them? You mean with a gun?"

"Yes, with a gun. When we go in, I'll make everybody get on the floor, then I'll go behind the teller's windows. I'll gather the money from each cash drawer and come back out. You'll grab billfolds and purses from the customers, and then we'll leave. It's simple."

"I don't know."

"I'm sorry Frances, but you need to do this for us, and Mikey, or you'll have to leave. Everybody has to pull their share of the load. We're in trouble and need help. If you love me, you'll help provide for our future. If you won't, there's a girl I met in town who I think will help us."

Through tears Frances blubbered. "I don't know. I'm so confused. Alright, I'll try."

"You'll have a .38 caliber revolver. It's loaded and has six shots. Have you ever shot a gun?"

"A .22 single shot rifle and a 12 gauge shotgun."

"A pistol is about the same thing. Just point at the target, aim, and pull the trigger. With a pistol you'll need to be within about ten feet of what you want to hit. But this is a piece of cake, and you won't have to shoot. Mikey and I haven't shot at anyone. He said we only need to carry guns to scare people, so they'll do what we tell them."

Michael chose one of the three cars and used a bent piece of coat hanger wire to lift the door lock post. While he hotwired the Hudson sedan, she transferred a cloth bag and two men's hats to the center of the bench seat. The bag was heavy. Frances looked inside and found two pistols and nylon stockings. Michael took time to show her how to put the nylon on her head, rolled up to fit under the man's hat. He hugged and kissed her. "If we need to talk, you're Cain and I'm Able. Be careful, don't get excited and use our real names."

The big six-cylinder inline engine started with a roar and in three minutes they were in town. Frances didn't ask, but assumed the cars belonged to workers who rode together to a job in another town. She'd known of a few people back home who did that.

At the city limits, a sign said they'd entered the town of Fulks. After four blocks, they were in the business section which was only two blocks long. At the end of the first block, Frances saw a clock hanging on the corner of a two-story brick building. A sign said it was The First State Bank of Calhoun County.

Michael pulled up to the curb and stopped but left the engine run. They stood by the car for half a minute while he checked up and down the street. No policemen or police cars were in sight. He nodded for Frances to go to the big oak double doors. On the sidewalk he told her, "While I'm behind the teller's counter, you remember to grab women's purses and men's billfolds."

There were two sets of doors at the entrance. They stopped between the doors and raised the hats to roll the nylons down over their faces. Michael said, "Follow me," then he pushed the inner doors open violently. "This is a holdup! Get on the floor or get shot." Frances took her place, stood in the middle of the customer area near a service table, and slowly waved her gun back and forth as four adults took positions on the floor. A woman in her mid-twenties struggled to control two young children and get them to sit still beside her.

Frances glanced around, in awe of the polished dark wood, shiny brass, and marble stone. It was the most beautiful thing she'd ever seen. Mother had never allowed her to go into the bank at home. Frances always had to wait outside in the truck and look through the big front window. She knew the marble floor would be cold on bare feet. It would sure beat the feel of warm mud, cow pies, and chicken droppings squeezed up between her toes.

Michael kicked a locked wood swing door open to enter the teller's area and the noise startled her. The wood splintered and the door panel hung by a single hinge. She heard him say, "Get down bitch." Michael's hand rose before he hit the teller hard and knocked her backward out of sight.

Frances took a man's billfold and heard another man's voice from the teller's cage.

"Who the hell do you think you are? Get out of my bank or I'll call the police."

She watched as Michael strode quickly to the bald, heavyset man and hit him in the face with the pistol butt. The man yelled and protested as Michael hit him twice more before he fell to the floor. From the body actions Michael made she knew he was kicking and stomping the man. The tellers cried out and one screamed.

Michael turned to the tellers below the counter. "Give me your jewelry and your purses." He moved along the cash drawers scooping all the bills and big silver change into a cloth bag.

He exited the teller's cage and yelled to Frances "Come on, Cain, let's go." She'd only gotten billfolds from three men and Michael put them in the bag.

They ran to the outer doors, where Michael stopped her. "Pull the nylon off your head and put it in your pants pocket with the gun, then walk casually to the car. Go ahead of me."

Michael followed her and they got in the car. He backed the car out cautiously and drove on through town. Frances was still afraid they'd get caught or be shot and killed. She huddled in the gray cloth seat and watched the side mirror for a police car. Three blocks down the street Michael turned right, drove two blocks and turned right again.

Near the edge of town where they'd entered, Michael cut back to the highway and drove back to the side road where they'd left the pickup. He jumped from the car and yelled, "Yaaahooo! We did it, you were great." He hugged and kissed Frances and told her she was a good bank robber, and he was proud to have her be his girlfriend. They quickly removed the hats, and he changed his shirt. She had her shoes and pants off when he motioned for her to get in the truck. He drove slowly toward Fulks while she finished changing clothes and brushed out her hair with her fingers. "Empty those billfolds of the money," Michael said, "and toss them out the window. Put your man's clothes under the seat and smile and relax."

They drove through town again, right past the bank where a lone police car was parked with the bubble gum machine on top flashing its single red light. A crowd had gathered around the bank entrance, but no one paid them any attention. Frances leaned back and exhaled a deep breath. Michael grinned. "See, I told you it was easy. Nothing to it."

Finally, she could relax and laugh; she was a bank robber, and she had a boyfriend. It took an hour and a half for her to calm down, but she was still high on the new excitement in her life.

She'd found a boyfriend who loved her and robbed banks.

Michael put his hand on her leg and slid it up her thigh. "In about thirty minutes we'll do it again. There's another bank up ahead. You need to change into your disguise again and be ready. She started to object but was captivated by his smile and self-confidence. *What the heck, I did it once and it wasn't bad. It's for us, me and my man.*

On the south end of town, they entered the parking lot of a small manufacturing plant. The truck was left at the end of a row of cars, out of sight of the guard shack. Michael had told her earlier that he'd checked and learned the guards only manned the shack for thirty minutes before and after shift changes. He chose a blue two-door Pontiac sedan. He opened the locked door then checked under the hood to ensure it had the straight eight-cylinder engine. Before he had it started, Frances had their equipment in the car. She was excited. She was eager to do it again.

The next town he'd picked was much bigger and looked more prosperous. Two banks sat at opposite corners in the middle of a larger business district. He left the car running in a deliveries only space and they walked to the bank's double doors to follow the same procedure. She saw a brass plaque with the name Madison County Farmer's Bank beside the doors. While they rolled the stockings down, he said, "There's a guard in this bank, get to him quick and keep an eye on him. He'll be in a chair against the left wall. Don't let him stand up and make him keep his hands in the air until I'm done behind the counter. And watch for more customers coming in. Make them get on the floor."

She was stunned. Before she could react, Michael flung the door open and yelled at the people that he was robbing the bank. She followed him and went straight to the guard with her arm outstretched and the gun pointed at his chest. "Get your hands up and keep them up." The older uniformed man had stood when they entered. His right hand was close to his gun, almost touching it. Slowly he raised his arms and sat back down in the wooden chair. He gave her a hard look but didn't appear fearful. Frances heard Michael yell at the tellers. She glanced toward Michael and counted six teller's windows. The customers had done what they were told and either sat or laid on the floor. Some looked frightened while others stared at Frances with looks of fearful loathing.

The guard was sixty or older. His black uniform was clean and had probably been freshly pressed. Likely by his wife she'd bet. He was a little overweight, maybe twenty pounds. His complexion was ruddy under white hair. She thought he looked like a nice man. While watching the guard, she stepped six paces to a man lying on his stomach and asked for his billfold. As he handed it to her she shifted her eyes and stooped to take it. Behind her she heard the entrance door open and shoes clicking on the marble floor.

At the edge of her vision Frances saw movement in the guard's direction. The woman who'd entered the bank screamed. The guard stood as his hand lunged down to his gun. Frances rose, glanced at the screaming woman and plunged forward toward the guard. His palm touched the gun in its holster. His fingers wrapped around the butt and raised it from the leather. The barrel rose toward her. Frances closed on him and pulled the trigger from four feet away and pulled it again and again. The guard stumbled backward, fell on the chair, knocked it over, and sprawled on the cold marble floor on his back. His eyes were open, and he stared unseeing at the ceiling. Blood left dark wet spots on his white shirt and jacket. Frances was sure he wasn't breathing. A man on the floor yelled curse words at her. Two women screamed while Frances froze, not sure of what to do. *I think I just killed a man. He fell hard and there's blood flowing from his chest. He looks dead. He hasn't moved.* Seconds later Michael grabbed her and pushed her toward the door. He spoke to her, but she didn't absorb what he said.

Outside several people had heard the gunshots and were cautiously walking toward the bank. Frances knew she had to get in the car if they were to escape. Michael fired two shots over the heads of the townspeople to frighten them. Frances jumped and cried out at the unexpected noise. The people scattered. Frances ran to the car.

Michael opened the passenger door and pushed Frances inside. As he opened the driver's door, he fired another round into the air.

Frances watched the driver's door open and then heard two more gunshots. A young man in a suit stood in the banks entrance with a pistol pointed at them. Another gun shot, closer than the others, was followed by a second. The young man dropped his gun to the pavement and staggered backward and then fell backward into the building. Frances had seen two red spots appear on the young man's white shirt. Michael jumped in the car. "God Damn it. That bastard tried to shoot me. I hope he's dead. I think he is."

In a rush, Michael squalled the tires as he quickly backed the car into the street. An oncoming car couldn't stop fast enough, and the Pontiac hit the other car's front right fender with a loud crunching of metal. The car shook from the jolt. Frances jumped and whimpered then cowered in the seat. At first, she feared they'd been shot at again. With a roar Michael raced down the street weaving to pass slower traffic in his way. In a minute they were in the residential area at the edge of town. He doubled back and again calmly drove toward the end of town where they'd entered. Michael removed his hat and threw it and the nylon out the window, then reached over and snatched Frances' hat and nylon and tossed them out, too. Driving with one hand he slapped her face to get her attention. "We're near the edge of town, change your clothes. Now. Damn it to hell, hurry." His voice was harsh, not kindly and friendly like before.

Later, when they'd exchanged the Pontiac for the Studebaker truck, they drove back through town like they had in Fulks. Before they got near the banks, they saw police cars parked in the street and patrolmen directing traffic around the blocks where the two banks sat. An ambulance was double parked with its lights flashing.

Frances stared straight ahead at nothing. Her face was pale and her breathing shallow. She was numb. She'd killed a man. Not just any man but a guard. The police would search especially hard for her because the guard was like one of them. The man looked like a nice person, but his death didn't concern her as much as the thought that she and Michael might be caught or shot. Earlier she'd been happier than at any time in her life. Now everything was upside down. She was mainly sorry she had failed Michael. As Mother would have predicted she'd screwed up her part. Then she had a sobering thought. Michael had shot a man too. Maybe he was dead also. They were both murdering bank robbers.

Outside town they drove in silence for almost an hour until they approached a roadhouse beside the oil and chip country road. Michael said he'd planned a circuitous route back to the farm to stay far from towns near the banks they'd robbed. He pulled in and parked, then casually walked inside. Through a window Frances watched him chug a beer while he stood talking to the man behind the bar. The bartender slid another beer across the wood bar. When Michael walked out he had a six-pack of longneck beer bottles under his arm.

In the truck he said, "Here drink all of this." He started the truck and pulled onto the highway. When she'd emptied the beer, he tossed the bottle out the window and handed her another. "Drink this one slowly while we talk."

"Talk? I just killed a stranger in the bank. And you likely killed a man, too. You said that wouldn't happen."

"Yeah, we shot them, but there wasn't any choice. If the guard had gotten his gun out, he would have killed you. You told him to keep his hand away from his weapon, but he chose to be a hero. He made that choice, not you. And as far the guy shooting at me, I didn't have a choice either. If I didn't shoot him, he might have killed me."

"I guess you're right. But I'm still sorry it happened though because I let you down."

The truck slowed and Michael let it bounce along the rough ground at the side of the road then parked on the shoulder and shut off the engine. "You didn't let me down. You're new at this and the guard took a chance. And then the other guy decided to get involved and took a chance too. Come here, we need to be strong and stick together. I'm in love with you. I know it's quick, but that's how I feel. We're a good team. We should include marriage in our future and think of having a family. We're good together. Do you love me enough to marry me? I'm proposing."

Frances smiled. "Yes, oh yes, I do love you. You're the first person who's had faith in me. I'm sorry I shot the guard. I do love you and I want to be your wife. I'll be Mrs. Michael Smith."

"We can have the ceremony at the house and invite your mom and all your relatives."

"Mother, definitely won't be able to come, and I don't care about the others. Just you and Mikey will be enough."

Back on the road Michael said, "Take this bag and count the money. See how we did on your first bank jobs."

After counting it twice under the dim overhead light she told him, "There's about six thousand, three hundred twenty-two dollars, a lot of silver coins and the jewelry."

"That's great, we did good, real good. If there's an engagement ring in there it's for you. I only got to five cash drawers at the last bank or there'd be more. We're a damn good team. How about if we put fifty-five hundred dollars toward the farm and you can spend the other eight hundred twenty-two dollars and the silver on the house and new clothes for yourself?"

"Do you mean it? I'll have an engagement ring? And money to fix the house and buy clothes I like? That's more money than I thought I'd ever see at once in my whole life." She closed her eyes and wallowed in her newfound good fortune. A smile formed and she leaned back to bask in the newness of her love for Michael. A faint, knowing smirk played across Michael's features as he stared straight ahead at the road.

Before they crested a hill at late dusk, Michael saw a red glow ahead. Frances had closed her eyes to think of what she would buy and fell asleep. Two police cars blocked the highway a quarter mile ahead with red lights flashing. As Michael eased off the gas and let the truck coast, he shook Frances. "Police roadblock up ahead! Grab the clothes you wore earlier and shove them under your dress. Smooth them out to look like you're pregnant. Slouch in the seat and push your belly out like you're ready to drop a baby at any minute." He grabbed the money bag and shoved it under his seat. They had thrown the beer bottles out as they emptied them and had one left. Cautiously he held it outside near his door and let it drop to the pavement.

Two State Troopers stood beside the cars, one carried a rifle, the other had a shotgun. A third man sat in a patrol car. Michael stopped beside the nearest Trooper as he walked toward them on the center line.

"What's up officer?"

"A couple of guys robbed two banks earlier today, shot and killed two men. May I see your license?"

"Sure." As Michael reached toward his right back pocket his hand brushed the handle of the revolver in the seat at his hip.

The officer squatted slightly and glanced at Frances in the dim light cast by the instrument panel. He saw her puffed up belly and uncomfortable frightened expression. "Never mind sir. In the condition your wife's in, there's no way she could be one of the people we want. Sorry to have inconvenienced you. Good night and good luck, ma'am."

He turned his attention back to Michael. "Sir, there's a law against drinking while you drive. Don't be dropping beer bottles out the window. We're not blind or stupid. I'm only letting you go without a ticket because of your wife's condition. Please drive carefully and obey the laws, sir."

The officer walked to the front of the truck in the glare of the headlamps and waved for the trooper in the patrol car to back onto the shoulder to let them pass. Michael moved his right hand to the gear shift lever, put the old truck in gear and eased through the roadblock. After a few hundred feet, when he'd shifted into fourth gear, both breathed deeply in relief. Then he placed his hand on Frances's leg. "Well mother-to-be, you got us out of that." His laughter was contagious. She started laughing with him, but nervously.

"Looks like dressing you up as a man worked. They're looking for two men robbers, not a Bonnie and Clyde duo. Don't that beat all? It's almost fully dark and I bet you're starved. I've been so wound up I forgot we haven't eaten since breakfast."

"Yes, I guess I am hungry. In all the excitement I hadn't noticed it either."

"There's a honky-tonk ahead about two or three miles as I recollect, we'll stop there. We've got a lot to celebrate tonight. Do you dance?"

"Dance? Sure, I've danced at weddings. I've never been to a honky-tonk. I've heard of them, but Mother would never allow me to be seen in one."

"Well, your Mother won't have anything to say about it tonight."

"You're right. Mother won't ever have anything to say about anything I do again."

Michael noticed Frances had a smiley, smirky expression as if she'd just said something funny.

"Good. We'll have dinner and a couple beers and a shot of whiskey to relax after that last scare. Then I'll dance with my fiancée."

Frances dug through the cloth bag until she found a wedding ring. It was too small for her stubby ring finger but fit her little pinky finger.

After they'd drank several beers and eaten fried steaks and potatoes and biscuits they danced. Michael held her close and whispered that he loved her.

Frances thought about Michael as he drove them home in the dark. *He's fifteen years older and much more experienced in everything. He's also a skilled lover. He knows just where to touch me and what to say to push me up to heaven. He even had me get on top of him, instead of underneath. Soon I'll be married, and we'll have children. Maybe I'll have another son, only this time I won't have to lie and say it was stillborn.*

Money, I didn't know there was so much money. Eight hundred and twenty-two dollars. All mine. I can buy new clothes and shoes. A hat! I'll buy a new beautiful hat, one with flowers and feathers on it. I'll need that since there'll be no more ugly hand-me-down hats from Mother.

Frances giggled out loud. *Mother would have a fit if she knew I had robbed a bank! An even bigger fit than if she learned I slept with a man after I only knew him for an afternoon. But the guard: Mother would get the leather strap and beat me if she knew I'd killed a man. Then she'd get the Sherriff and turn both of us in as murderers. She'd do that to her own daughter and future son-in-law. I know she would have, damn her.*

They reached the farm long after dark and went straight upstairs to Michael's room. She loved Michael's attention. She'd only had sex three times before him. She recalled her first time with pimple faced Willie Frankle. He actually thanked her when they were done. Said it was his first time too. Then he apologized in case he'd hurt her.

She was so happy she'd even accepted and rationalized it was all right to shoot the guard they were sure she'd killed. He had it coming for trying to stop them. It wasn't like she didn't warn him. And the man Michael shot started it by shooting at them.

The next morning when they rose Michael cuddled her and had sex again. He dressed and went outside while she made the bed. In the kitchen she prepared breakfast for her man.

Frances saw Michael behind the kitchen and went outside to tell him the food was ready. He'd been hunting rabbits with a Savage .410 caliber pump shotgun. She saw two rabbits, skinned and gutted. He was ready to cut them into pieces to soak the meat in salt water. "Look what I got," He said with obvious pride, "Fresh rabbits for supper."

"Mother always said not to eat them except when it was cool out. She said they carry a fever and can make people sick in hot weather."

He gave her a harsh look and raised his voice. "Your Mother must be ignorant. I've eat rabbits year round all my life and it hasn't hurt me. You'll cook these for supper because I'm telling you to, and I don't want to hear any more crap about it." He turned away from her and finished dressing the fresh game. Frances was unsure of what to say and went back inside.

For their lunch she made bologna sandwiches, sliced tomatoes, and cucumbers in sweetened vinegar. They ate in silence. Michael was once again distant and sullen. Afterward she watered the few plants remaining in the garden and picked the last of the leaf lettuce, more tomatoes, and cucumbers for a salad. Mother had taught her to make salad dressing, and she found all the ingredients to fix it. She browned and simmered the rabbits for dinner and planned to serve them with sliced fried potatoes and the salad to surprise Michael. He was still distant, but not as grouchy as he'd been at lunch. She decided she'd try to be careful about what she said and not antagonize him again.

They ate at six, and later she washed and dried the dishes. She heard Michael snoring in the living room. She was happy and sang softly while she finished in the kitchen.

Frances was bored and Michael was still asleep, so she roamed the house again; then she decided to impress Michael. She'd make him a special supper the next night. She found little in the refrigerator and went to the freezer in the pantry. The big twenty cubic foot Kelvinator chest freezer was full to the top with frozen food, mostly meat. She rummaged around moving white freezer paper packages looking for just the right item to cook for supper.

After she'd moved a few more packages others slid aside. Her eyes widened, her gut tightened, and she screamed. A man's face stared up at her. The eyes were open, and the chubby features were covered with frost. She was mesmerized by a dark indentation in his forehead. His hair was brown and thin, and he needed a shave. He wore a blue chambray work shirt, and his body had been folded and bent to fit inside the freezer box. She hesitated, fascinated by the terrible sight, and finally turned to run. Michael stood behind her with a sardonic grin on his face. He trapped her in his arms. "Miss Frances say hello to your Cousin Mikey."

Frances struggled to get loose, twisted away from Michael's grasp, slapped his face and attempted to run. Michael hit her on the shoulder with his fist and she lurched into the table. Before she could escape, he caught her and twisted her right arm behind her. He pushed her to the parlor, then toward the stairs. On the way through the parlor, he leaned down and grabbed the coiled rope from the corner.

In her room, Frances resisted and broke free of his grasp. She hit him and scratched his face until he cursed then hit her in the stomach with his fist. She folded and dropped to the floor gagging and clutching her abdomen. He ripped her clothes away, dragged her onto the bed, then tied her hands to the iron headboard rods. Silently he raped her. He was violent and fast. It was a complete change from their previous love making sessions.

Frances was confused by the sight of the body in the freezer and Michael's transformation. One minute they were lovers and the next he had forced himself on her and took what he wanted. Fear had taken over when she found the body and it had steadily grown stronger as he brutally violated her. She cringed when she remembered him saying the man in the freezer was her Cousin Mikey.

After he silently moved away from her, he put his shorts and undershirt on. He left her tied to the bed and sat on a chair next to it. He grinned wryly as he slipped his thumbs through the straps on this undershirt.

"Sorry you found Mikey. I had it in my mind to keep you around for another day or two. Now that's got to change." He snorted. "I'm not a partner in this piece of crap farm, and my names not Michael or Smith. If that damned trooper had read my driver's license last night you would have learned what my name really is. But it really wouldn't have mattered in the end.

"I was traveling the area checking banks when I met that moron cousin of yours. He was crying in his beer at the tavern in town and said he'd do anything to save his farm. The mortgage on this poor piece of ground is more than it's worth. Mikey was too stupid and lazy to be a successful farmer. I know because I was raised on a farm where my daddy and brothers made money. Although for the past few years everybody has lost money because of the drought.

"Anyway, this season's wheat harvest was so bad there weren't enough money for Mikey to make the payment on the loan at the bank. I convinced him to help me rob some banks. We were partners in that sense, but it wasn't his idea. He was too stupid to think of anything like that. After three robberies he turned chicken and wanted to quit. He wanted to put his share of the money into this pathetic piece of dirt."

Frances couldn't sit up the way she was tied. She crossed her ankles, put her legs together, clamped them tight, and listened horrified.

"Eventually we fell into a falling out and I killed him. I had him go outside to look at the well pump then called to him. When he turned to look at me, I shot him in the forehead. When he'd bled out, I put him in the freezer. I'm not a gravedigger, it's too much work, especially in this heat and with the dry ground as hard as rock. Emptying and refilling that big freezer box was enough work. Your cousin was a failure as a farmer, and almost as useless as a thief. I never intended to split the money with him anyway. But I had planned for him to help me rob several more banks before I moved on." Michael smiled widely. "That's when you came in."

"You didn't have to kill him. You could have just taken the money and left. He couldn't turn you in to the Sherriff or he'd have gone to jail, too."

"Frances, haven't you heard a word I've said? Put two and two together and Mikey was stupid enough to do just that. If he couldn't save his beloved piece of dirt and this crappy old house, he would have turned me in just to get even. Besides, it doesn't bother me to kill people, as you'll soon learn. It's really not a big deal, just like that guy outside the bank yesterday. I didn't lose any sleep over him. You know what I mean, you did it and it doesn't appear to bother you much."

She stared at him wide-eyed, and her fear ratcheted up another notch. "Did you just imply you were going to kill me? You said you loved me and we would be married. Why would you kill me?"

"Because I want to." Michael stood and leaned over Frances.

"As for the money, I can live for over a year on what I had before you arrived. When you showed up I tried to run you off. Then I started to think about whether to kill you right then and move on or decide if I could use you. You turned out to be Mikey's replacement. Stupidity must run in your family. All I had to do was get some beer in you and put on a phony act to seduce you so you'd be my new partner. With the money we got yesterday I've got enough cash to live real good for more than two years, by myself, that is."

Frances was upset. "You said all those nice things and treated me good just so I'd help you rob banks? You even proposed marriage and said you wanted a family. You're a no-good lying bastard."

"Yeah, that I am. I only intended to keep you around for five or six days at the most anyway." Michael turned somber. "But it's your fault that guard got shot. If you'd done your end right and kept the drop on him, he wouldn't have tried to draw on you. Then I could have disarmed him and knocked him out. But truthfully, even if I'd done that the other young guy might still have come gunning for us anyway. Since the cops are looking for two men, I need to travel by myself and then I won't be noticed.

"So you see Frances, I'd planned to kill you in a few days anyway because I've done enough bank jobs in this area. Now with two men dead and you finding Mikey it's time for me to move on. I've just moved my schedule ahead some since you got nosey." He grinned and laughed.

Tears streamed down her face. "Take me with you please, I won't tell anyone what we did," she begged. "Please don't kill me."

He grinned at her evilly. Frances saw cruel meanness in his eyes. "Go ahead and beg. I like that, it shows how pathetic, weak, and stupid you are. You just don't understand that I like to kill people, especially women when there's time to do it right.

"Why do I think you're stupid? Because you fell for me so hard you hopped right in bed the first day we met, just like a good little whore. Then you agreed to help rob a bank because you were so deeply in love after a few good screws. Huh, good screws. It was good for you, but mediocre for me. You're actually pathetic at sex. Look at yourself. You're fat, ugly, and stupid. What man would love you? I'll continue to have sex with you because you're the only thing here, but that doesn't mean I'd want you around forever. I'd about as soon have a damn sheep as you. In fact, I couldn't stand to listen to you, or look at you for a full week."

He stood and removed his underwear.

"No, you're not going to do me again. I don't want you."

He climbed on top of her. "Shut up or I'll hurt you and give you something else to complain about."

"No, damn you, you're never going to do me again." She began to twist and bounce, attempting to throw him off. Instead, he rose above her and punched her on the side of the head. She continued to fight him. He forced his face to hers and grabbed her bottom lip with his teeth then jerked his head. Blood flowed from the torn lip and he laughed while he sucked and licked the blood from the wound as she cried and whimpered.

When he finished with her, he got off and began to slap and punch her body all over in a violent fit. Finally, he backed away and stared at her with a sadistic grin. "I'm thinking about what I'm going to do to you before I leave. When I go down, I'll gather the tools from the kitchen and the equipment shed I'll need to work on you."

Abruptly he dressed and left the room. She was terrified. In the silent dimness she thought of him and home. *I've got to fight back to get away from him. I need to get really angry, like I did with Mother. That damned Thornton boy, Jacob. It was only my third time having sex and he got me pregnant. When my belly showed, Mother called me a whore, a dirty slut, a filthy pig and other mean names. God that made me mad. She made me quit school before my senior year started and wouldn't let me leave the farm. She even made me hide upstairs when visitors dropped in. When the baby was born she didn't offer to help me and I had to deliver it myself. I told Mother it was a stillbirth. Two days later I dug a grave out behind the barn and buried the little bastard I'd suffocated. I'll have to get that mad at*

*Michael. He enjoys my fear of him
while I beg for my life.*

*I wish my daddy was here to fight
for me. He was a good man and
protected me from Mother. He
wouldn't let her hit me with the leather
strap. I heard him tell Mother that in
his opinion I needed more love, not
punishment. But he up and died with
the TB.*

Frances heard shoes stomp on the
stairs.

Michael returned with four beers as
if nothing had changed between them.
"Looks like this beer is going to be
your last meal cause I ain't cookin for
you. If you behave, I'll untie you while
we drink and talk some more. But if
you make me mad, I'll tie you up again
and really hurt you before I kill you.
You don't know it yet, but there are
worse things than simply dying." He
untied her and sat on the straight chair
while she sat on the edge of the bed.

"Please Michael don't— Michael slapped her viciously.

"Shut up, damn it. I want you to know you won't be the first woman I've killed. I like to rape and murder women. I wish there was time to kill you properly, so I could listen to your screams and see the fear and pain in your eyes. That's where the real pleasure is. I'd like to watch your eyes when you realize you're going to die and see hope fade as you accept there's no escape. That would make up for me having to act like I cared for you these past few days.

"I've decided to leave tonight and hide further south. The police will soon find the remains of you and Mikey, and I want to be far away when they do."

Frances was shocked by his revelations. She knew he wouldn't tell her those things about himself unless he was confident she couldn't escape.

He was enjoying her fear and begging while he taunted her. "Please Michael, I'll just move on and find a job somewhere and disappear. I won't cause you any trouble, I promise. I can't say anything to anybody because they'd put me in prison for murdering that guard."

"Don't whine. You're going to die before I leave and that's final. I've only come to talk to you to kill time until later tonight because I'm not sleepy yet."

"So everything you told me was lies. You play acted and led me on just so you would have a partner to rob a bank? Was anything true or was it all lies?"

Michael turned sullen, "You noticed there weren't any livestock on the farm. I lied about that too. The cows needed to be milked and them and the horses needed to be watered and fed every day. I'm not into this farming crap, so I took them all to the end of the pasture as far from the house as I could get and shot them. Luckily the wind blows mostly out of the southwest, so the stench isn't carried to the house."

"You're cruel and evil if you can kill poor dumb animals like that and laugh about it."

"Why not laugh about it? I kill poor dumb animals like you and your stupid cousin and laugh about it." Michael leaned forward with his hands on both knees. "The other day you mentioned there weren't any cats and dogs around. Some left when they didn't get fed or watered and I used the others for target practice. I'm a good shot; but a man needs to practice to stay good. And that story about being in the Army? It was a lie, too. I couldn't put up with that taking orders crap for a single day. There wasn't any money from mustering out pay and I sure as hell wouldn't have put any money of mine in this damned run-down piece of worn-out ground. Oh, and I've also never been married. If I had been and a bitch cheated on me, you can bet your ass there'd be pieces of her scattered across ten counties when I was finished working on her ass."

Near dark Michael retied Frances' hands to the bed. "Open your hand," he commanded. When her fingers were straight he slipped the small diamond ring off her pinky finger. He picked up her suitcase, turned the light off and closed the door. After he crossed the hall, she heard bed springs creak as he laid down.

She couldn't sleep. She dreaded to think about what he might do to her and what the tools were that he said he would use. Her lip hurt where he'd ripped it. She could feel the loose flap of flesh with her tongue and felt where the blood had run down her chin and onto her chest and dried. Her whole body ached from the pounding he'd given her in a hateful frenzy. *He's not tender and loving with me like at first. I've finally accepted it was all an act. I was lied to and fell for him just as he'd planned. He judged me to be a stupid young girl and used me. He even said I was worthless in bed. Mother was right damn it. I am stupid. I see things that I overlooked at the start, but it's too late now. He didn't look like a farmer. His hands, forearms and face were much lighter tanned than people who worked the fields regularly. The rest of him is as white as my butt. And his hands are soft, not rough and calloused. Most farmers' fingers are split open on the ends from working in dry dirt and dust.* Frances couldn't sleep. She tossed and turned and tried to pull the ropes loose.

Much later, she heard Michael rise from the bed and go downstairs. She judged it was well past midnight. Then she heard his footsteps again. She pulled against the ropes, but the knots held. He flung the door open and stood in the doorframe. Light from the small hall fixture cast an eerie glow behind him. She thought of the way the preacher at the Baptist church had described Satan. Reaching along the wall Michael flipped the light on and then untied her hands.

"Get off the bed and stand with your back to me. Now, damn it, move your fat ass."

Still naked, she did as she was told, but he slapped her hard on her ass cheeks anyway.

"Please don't hurt me. I'll do anything you want if you take me with you." He laughed and didn't answer while he tied a loop in the end of the piece of rope and placed it over her head. She shook as he tightened it against her neck.

He forced her to go down the stairs first, then they walked to the barn by the light of a kerosene lantern he carried. She whined and complained as she stepped on rocks in the driveway and was pushed from behind. She hadn't been to the outhouse for hours and her bladder ached from the beers she'd drank.

A year-old shiny black Dodge two door sedan sat inside the barn. "Like the car? It's mine, the only possession I have. I paid cash for it with money from last year's bank jobs. I'll leave in it in an hour. I've already got the money and everything else of mine packed in the trunk. When I say mine, I've included your share of the bank money and the hundred dollars or so from your suitcase. That cheap battered old thing and your clothes are in here to burn with you."

"Why are you doing this, Michael? I love you. I'll do anything for you."

Frances smelled kerosene vapors mingled in the air. Two red five-gallon fuel cans were on the dirt floor, on their sides with the caps off. She realized he'd told her the truth about burning the barn with her in it. She dreaded to think of what else he might do to her before he left.

Michael smiled evilly as he turned his gaze away from her. She turned to where he was staring and saw the tools from the kitchen and the shed he talked about: a long sharp filleting knife, a meat fork, pliers and a ball peen hammer. As he turned away she moved her feet apart and felt warm liquid flow down her legs as her whole body quivered and shook with fear.

Over his shoulder he said, "But I don't love you, Frances. I never did and never would. I don't even like you as much as the livestock I killed."

He tied the rope around her neck to a post before he put the lantern on the floor and lit another. He walked away then climbed to the loft where bedding straw was stored. The ladder he climbed was made of 2 x 4 pieces of lumber nailed to the studs of the tack room. A square hole was cut in the deck boards of the loft above for the ladder to extend through.

Frances noticed the barn differed from Mother's. A loft ran down each side of the building with straw on the left and hay on the right. The twelve-foot-wide middle section between the lofts was open to the roof. Near the peak of the roof a steel beam ran the length of the barn. A trolley hung from the beam and a block and tackle dropped from it to a hay tong. A tack room and three livestock stalls were under the left loft and six stalls with milking stations were on the right. She dreaded to think of what would happen to her if she climbed up there with Michael. She had to escape and save herself. She could do that. She had no other choice.

Michael left the lantern on the loft deck and returned to the barn floor. He left the rope tied to the post and cut it at the post. He went up the ladder and made her climb it after him. The narrow boards hurt her feet when she stepped on them. When she resisted, he yanked hard on the rope and choked her.

When she stood on the loft deck the smell of kerosene was even stronger. She saw the dark areas in the straw where the fuel had been poured. Michael removed the rope from her neck. She'd talked herself into hating him and hit him in the face and on his chest. He punched her in the stomach again and then on the jaw, knocking her down. She retched and her head hurt. He grinned and laughed at her feeble attack. He squatted over her, then tied her hands together in front of her before he threw the rope across an overhead beam. With her standing, he tied the rope off, out of her reach. He left slack in the line so she could attempt to evade him. He liked it when women fought back. It just added another reason to kill them.

He stepped in close behind her and ran his hands over her body, stopping at her breast. "You weren't the best lay I've ever had for damn sure, but I'll still miss your ass for a day or two until I find someone else. I'll take one last piece from you on the pile of loose straw before I shoot you." He laughed. "Or maybe I'll cut your throat when I'm done. Or better than that I may shoot your kneecaps and leave you alive to burn. I like the thought of that best, so that's what I'll do." He left the lantern on the floor at a spot kicked clear of straw six feet away from her.

He grinned broadly at the fear in her expression before he climbed down from the loft.

A short time later he returned through the barn doors with Mikey on his shoulder. The trolley on the beam squeaked when it moved as Michael pulled it to the center of the barn. He used the hay tongs attached to the block and tackle to haul the contorted, stiff body to the loft. He placed Mikey three feet from Frances on top of dry straw bales and tossed the set of heavy double steel tongs aside on the floor. He grinned as he breathed deeply. "Mikey should thaw fast with what I have planned for the two of you. I wanted him up here because the house will be rigged to catch fire shortly after I light the barn. If I'd left Mikey in the freezer he'd be protected and found there. I like the idea of cremating both of you together." Frances was terrified; she knew all too well what barn fires could do. Oh yes, she knew well. It had only been days since she'd seen one.

"Hauling Mikey out of the freezer and out to the barn made me hot and sweaty. I'm going back to the house to pack the last of the beer and food and finish setting it to burn, but I'll be right back in case you start to miss me." He laughed loudly as he left, taunting her again and enjoying the pained expression it wrought.

She heard him sing a country western tune "Sleepin At The Foot of The Bed" until it faded away outside the barn. She pulled the slack out of the line and brought her hands down to her chest. She had a plan. The line on her hands had enough slack that she might be able to reach a nearby pitchfork with her foot and pull it to her. She stood on one leg, stretched her body, leaned against the rope as far as she could stretch and hooked the pitchfork handle between her toes. The handle moved... she lost her grip and the handle fell back to the wall.

Frances took two deep breaths and tried again. The pitchfork fell toward her. She dropped her outstretched leg to the floor and wobbled as she straightened. The handle hit well above her belly button, and she bent to trap it with her elbows. By flexing her stomach muscles and pushing gently against the handle, she worked the end of the wood handle up her torso. Finally, her fingers touched the handle and worked it upward to her palms. Standing on one leg and with her other foot between the tines she raised her leg and lifted the handle so her hands could grip it tighter. She was nervous. If she dropped the pitchfork, there wouldn't be time to wrestle it back into her grasp again. It had to be done right the first time. She struggled and used both hands to turn the fork until the handle was on the floor and the tines were in her hands. She held the handle between her knees and forced a pointed tine through the first knot and wiggled the rope until the knot began to loosen. The knot was tight, and she forced and twisted it until it gave way. Blood flowed from her wrist where another sharp, pointed tine had scraped it. She moved the next knot to a tine and wiggled it until it came loose. Suddenly both hands were free. The pitchfork was thrust into a straw bale out of her way. She'd seen two four-foot-long pieces of 2 x 4 in the corner and grabbed one. Twice she swung it like a ball bat to get the feel of it. She wished it were heavier.

She heard a new sound; Michael whistled as he returned to the barn. There would only be one chance and she had to bring him down the first time. She crouched low where he'd ascend the ladder and waited for him to appear.

The car door slammed shut. What was he doing? Why was he taking so long? Noises below indicated he was moving and doing something, but what? She waited for the sound of his shoes to clack against the ladder rungs.

Finally, she heard the sounds of leather soles on wood. Then his head appeared in the floor opening. She tightened her grip on the cudgel, built up her determination, and waited. At the top of the ladder Michael turned his body so his left foot could reach the deck boards behind him. Frances put all her muscle and hatred into the swing and grunted as the narrow edge of the board connected with Michael's left upper arm. She heard the bone break. He grunted and lunged left to keep from falling down through the floor opening. He was doubled over on his knees and screamed as his left arm folded under him. His head turned toward her, and he frowned with a surprised look that quickly morphed to hatred.

Frances raised the board again and drove Michael down flat to the floor with four round house blows to his head. He laid on the deck semiconscious, on his stomach with his head hung over the edge of the loft. His left arm lay at an unnatural angle. She was pumped up with fear as she strained to lift the heavy cast steel hay tong and positioned it over Michael's midsection. He stirred and her fear drove her to move faster. She pulled on the live end of the rope to make the tongs grip his body and hauled him up. His body dragged through loose straw along the loft floor until it rose off the boards and swung out over the barn's alleyway.

Michael swung in the open space as Frances tied the line off. Conscious and in pain, he screamed at her. "Let me down from here right now you bitch. I'll get you for this." The more he struggled the tighter the sharp tongs gripped his flesh. With an evil smirk he reached with his right hand for the pistol in his pants waistband under his shirt.

Frightened of being shot, Frances grabbed the pitchfork handle in both hands, raised it high and stood at the edge of the loft. As the gun pulled clear Michael extended his arm, pointing the gun barrel in her direction as he swung and rotated at the end of the rope. He fired a shot and missed. Before the pistol lined up with her again, she swung the pitchfork down. The tines rustled through the silent air and lacerated his arm deeply from above his elbow to his wrist. Blood spurted from the deep tears, and Michael screamed louder as the gun was knocked from his grasp.

The tongs gripped Michael firmly from the back and held him horizontal. He swung freely and was powerless to release the steel claws. Frances used the fork to stab his body. She pushed Michael out and let him swing toward her, increasing his momentum with each jab. He attempted to divert the fork with his right hand but only got it pierced by the sharp, pointed tines. He continued to scream and curse her the whole time she attacked him. A maniacal grin spread across her features. "I'll show you pain you mean bastard."

Finally, as Michael's feet swung above and toward her with momentum, she jammed the five tines up into his stomach viciously with all her might. He was impaled and the pain and shock caused him to whimper and moan and then cry out in an agonized wail.

"You like pain, you bastard? You told me you did. Well, here's more." She continued to drive the fork further into his abdomen with vicious jabs until it was up to his ribs. Frances laughed as she shifted the handle up-and-down to hurt him as much as possible. She wanted to hurt him for the mean way she'd been treated and the threats he'd made about how he would make her suffer before he burned her. Michael's eyes rolled upward and bulged as he hung helpless. His arms, legs and head gradually lowered and pointed toward the dirt floor below.

Frances still feared him. He could still pose a danger. She scampered barefooted and naked down the ladder to retrieve the pistol. She was as least fifteen feet below him, frightened, and wasn't sure she could hit Michael's body as it gently swung and rotated. He had to be killed or he might still be a threat. He'd shown her no mercy and would get none from her.

Michael stared at her with hate in his eyes, but he no longer laughed or threatened her. She pulled the gate to a stall halfway open and stood near the top, balancing while trying to get closer. She fired the gun twice at his body. Michael jerked and yelled, but she feared the wounds weren't fatal. She wanted him dead. He had to die for her to feel safe.

Back on the loft she pulled the rope attached to the tongs toward her and tied the rope off. As his upper torso rotated toward her, she shot him in the head twice from three feet away. There was no doubt he was finally dead. She pulled him to the loft and attempted to drop the body next to her cousin among the straw bales. The positioning was awkward and difficult because the fork protruded down from his belly.

She grasped his hair to hold him in the position she wanted. His hair was slippery with blood, but she was determined to hold on as she lowered him with the other arm. His legs dropped toward the bales, but the fork was in the way. She released his hair and saw her hand was covered with blood. She wiped the hand on her leg then twisted the fork to the side while she lowered him further. Both legs landed on the bales and she tied him off, still almost three feet from the deck.

Frances reached for the pitchfork to pull it from Michael's body and realized she should have removed it while he was higher in the air. The tines were twisted and embedded tightly in his flesh.

The memory of another recent barn scene stole her attention as her mind drifted. Briefly she recalled how

Mother had yelled at her for sloppy milking just three days before. *The skinny old biddy grabbed me by the hair and pushed me away violently. Then she sat at the three-legged milking stool to finish the teat squeezing herself, berating me all the while. Mother had gone too far that time and I was sick of her abuse. The eighteen inch-long corn knife hung at the back of the barn where we used it to chop silage into pieces for feeding the cows. It was razor sharp. I had sharpened the blade on the grinding wheel the previous week. I was breathing fast and deep as I stood behind Mother while she continued to complain and run me down. I remember my lips quivered, my hands were sweaty, and the rest of my body felt clammy. I was nervous and afraid but enough was enough. I twisted my body like a coiled spring, then swung the knife and pulled it to me as it connected with Mother's neck. It almost cut her head clean off. The old biddy couldn't complain about the job not being done right that time. It was one of the few tasks she would have agreed I did well. I barely remember swinging the knife over and over, chopping and chopping her to pieces. Her blue pattern gingham dress was almost totally red when I finished.*

From the barn, I went to the house to pack my things. When I looked in a mirror I was covered with blood. After I washed and put on clean clothes, I found Cousin Mikey's mailing address and directions to his farm. Mother had it organized neatly in her writing desk. There was a hundred and thirteen dollars in Mother's metal farm money box, and I took all of it. I had earned it and deserved it.

Before leaving, I set fire to the barn and then drove off in the old Chevy pickup. When I stopped at the end of the lane an orange glow framed the old barn and smoke and fire shot through every crack and crevice. It was beautiful. Mother was in there, scattered in all her many pieces.

The fork pulled out of the suspended body after a tremendous downward yank on the handle. Frances's mind raced back to the present as she spun around with the momentum of her effort. Her bare feet slipped on the loose straw, and she turned in a circle while trying to regain her balance.

A movement close by on the loft surprised and frightened her. Michael's left leg slid off a hay bale; his shoe thumped onto the floor. *He's still alive!* The pitchfork was still in motion. The steel tines hit the lantern on the floor. The lantern crashed onto its side near the ladder opening, the mantle broke, and kerosene spilled. Loose straw on the floor ignited instantly. Flames rushed through the kerosene-soaked straw to her left and quickly raced up the pile of bales. Flames quickly surrounded the escape ladder. Surprise and fear showed on Frances's face as she jumped backward from Michael and the blaze. Both were after her. Thoughts of the other barn blaze flashed in her mind and Mother's image took shape in the spreading flames. Mother came at her, growing and frowning in the fire and smoke as she approached. Frances moved back and waved her arms to ward Mother off. "Go away, you're dead," She screamed.

Frances retreated to the edge of the loft until she teetered momentarily on the edge. She lost her balance and slowly fell backward. Her arms and legs flailed the air as she tried in vain to slow her fall. Mother seemed to smile as she watched from above.

Frances expected to land flat on the packed dirt floor. She would survive; she had fallen that far in the barn at home.

She suddenly remembered opening the gate to the horse stall below but not closing it. Twisting her neck to the left she saw the gate just before she landed hard on it. Her fall stopped short of the dirt floor as her lower back hit across the top board in line with the gate's vertical stiffener brace. The force of her descent bent her body backward; her head almost touched her feet. She'd never felt such intense pain as her stomach muscles ripped and the vertebras in her spine crushed and separated. It was far worse than delivering the baby boy. Her body bounced off the gate and rolled on the dirt floor. Coming to rest on her stomach, she saw the orange glow of flames and heard the crackle as fire raced through the straw above her. She knew she had to crawl to Michael's car, stand and leave.

Fear quickly enveloped her mind. Her legs wouldn't move! Her limbs refused to obey her thoughts. She had no feeling in her limbs. But then she felt her right hand move. Frances willed that hand to drag her away from the heat to safety. The nails on her hand ripped away from her fingers as she clawed at the hard dirt floor to make them pull her away from the smoke and heat. Her right cheek lay on the dirt, but her neck wouldn't turn her head. Her body refused her mind's command to rollover onto her back. She panicked and cried out. In front of her she saw Mother and heard maniacal laughter from the eerie image. Beside Mother floated three other frightful images.

Frances smelled hair burning and felt blisters forming on her left cheek and forehead. The increasing heat was unbearable. Sparks and embers of straw rained on and around her. Straw in the stalls in front of her was on fire. The inferno sucked oxygen through the open barn door with a roar and increased its temperature each second.

Frances suddenly accepted that her actions had condemned her to spend eternity under the wrath of the people she'd murdered: Mother, her bastard son, Michael and a stern bank guard. Before the smoke and searing heat silenced her, the last sounds Frances heard were her own hoarse screams as she saw visions of her future tormenters surrounding her in hell.

The End

Please return to your retailer to leave a review of 59 Hours.

Thank you. I hope you enjoyed this simple short story about the lives of two evil people.

Robert Schobernd

Robert and his wife, Addie, live in the USA northeast of St. Louis, Missouri, where he pursues his passion for writing.

69952398R00060